Falling Angels

COLIN THOMPSON

The first time Sally flew was before she could even crawl. As her parents slept, she floated above them, too young to speak, too young to think in words.

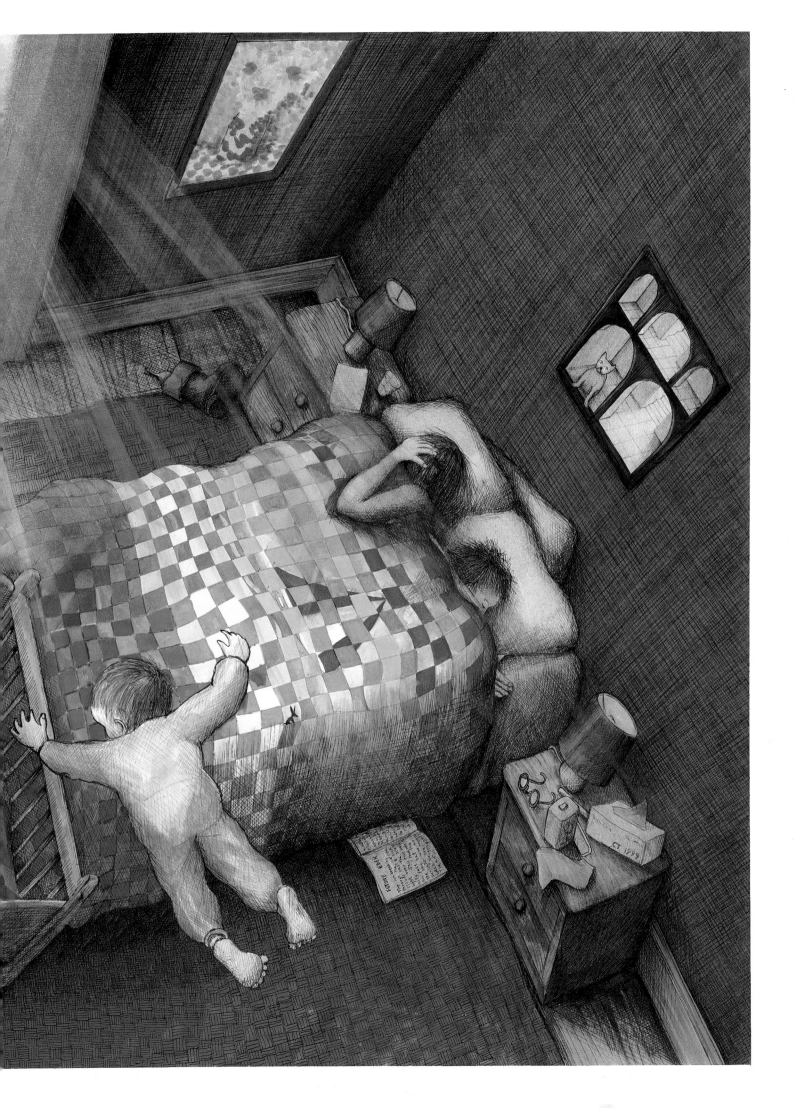

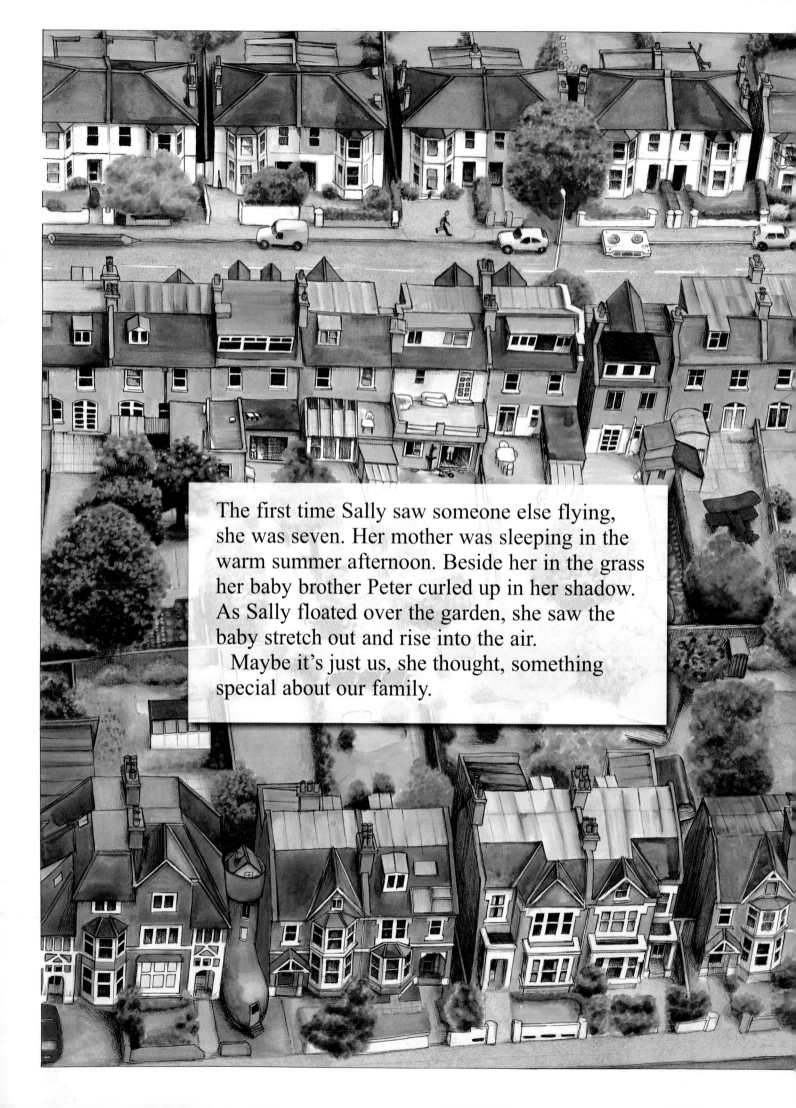

The first time Sally saw someone else flying, she was seven. Her mother was sleeping in the warm summer afternoon. Beside her in the grass her baby brother Peter curled up in her shadow. As Sally floated over the garden, she saw the baby stretch out and rise into the air.

Maybe it's just us, she thought, something special about our family.

As the years passed, Sally flew to wild and wonderful places, distant lands she had only seen in books. And in the afternoons she sat by her grandmother's bed and told her about everything she'd seen.

'You and your silly stories,' said her mother. 'It's time you came down to earth.'

'They're not stories,' said Sally when her mother had left the room.

Her grandmother just smiled.

I'll prove it, said Sally to herself, and the next morning, while everyone was still asleep, she flew into the heart of Africa. She watched the sun creep over the horizon and wake up the world for another day. She flew into the deepest part of the rainforest and in the branches of a great firewheel tree she found a beautiful orchid, which she took back to her grandmother.

The next day she flew to the desert and
brought her grandmother precious stones.

The day after, she flew to the shores of Patagonia and brought her grandmother a seashell.

It was the hottest summer anyone could remember. The air hummed with insects and was full of the scent of roses. Sally sat by the open window of her grandmother's room, trying to catch the breeze.

'Do you know what I would like to see once more before I die?' said the old lady.

'What?'

'The snow,' said the old lady.

So Sally slipped away to the bottom of the garden and flew north. She climbed up into the sky, higher than she had ever flown before. She followed the sun as it flowed round the world, turning the tops of the mountains into gold, until she reached the endless fields of snow.

And there in an enormous field of white where no one had ever walked, she touched the ground with the first human footsteps. She gathered up a ball of snow and flew home.

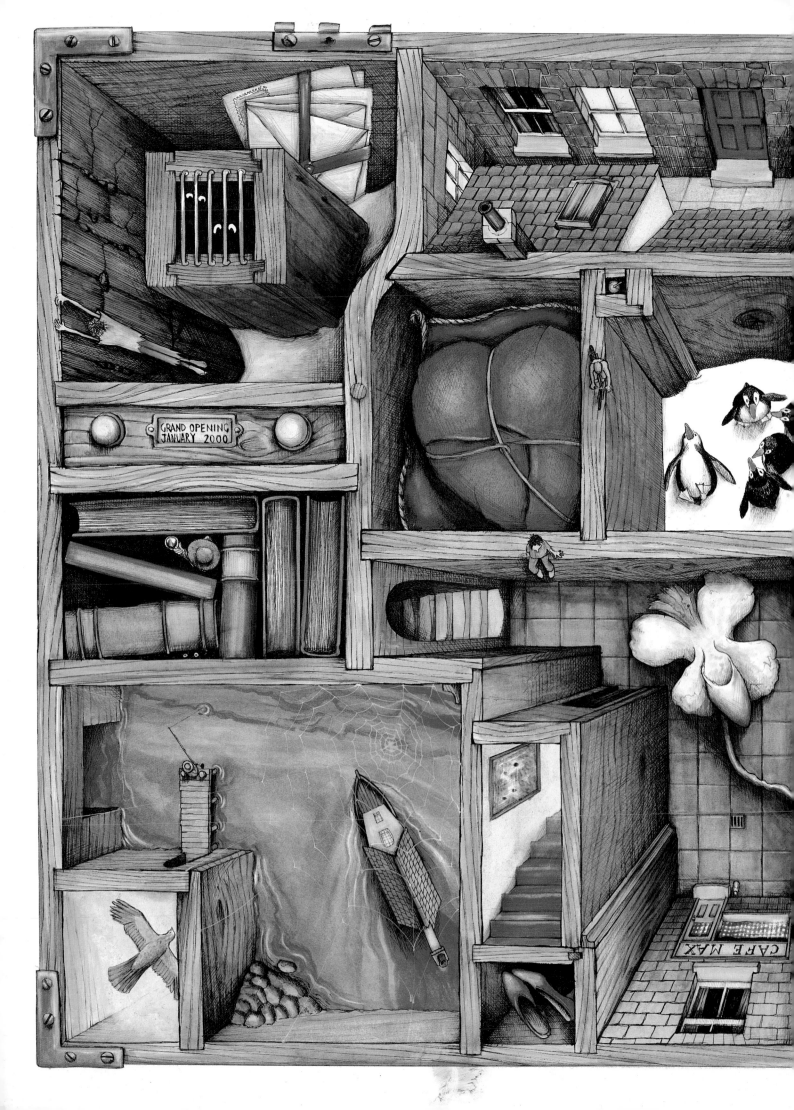

'Here, grandmother,' she said, handing the old lady the ball of snow.

Sally's grandmother pointed to a small box.

'Bring me that,' she said.

The box was divided into compartments. In one there was a dried orchid, in another, precious stones and in another, a lake.

'There's the snowball I brought my grandmother,' said the old lady.

'So you can fly too?' said Sally.

'Yes.'

'So why can't everyone do it?' Sally asked.

'Because they've forgotten how and once it's forgotten, it never comes back . . .'

THE LAST PICTURE OF THE TWENTIETH CENTURY

'Some people
see the world
with their
eyes.'

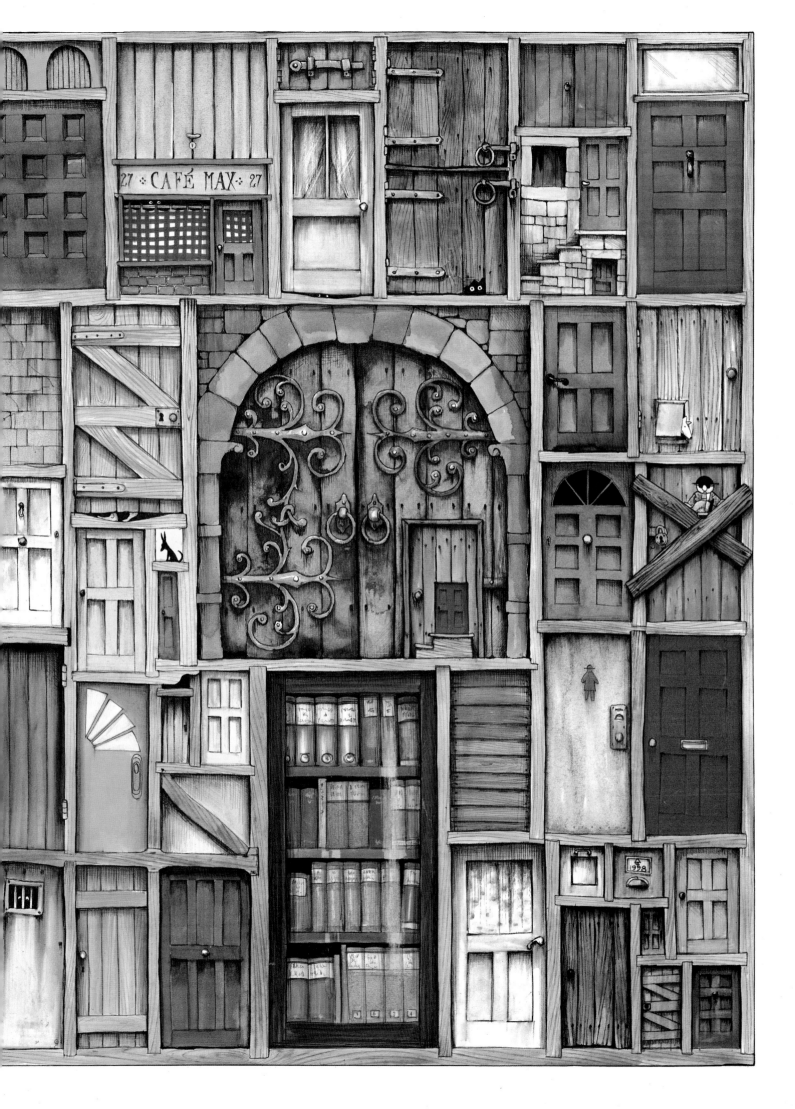

'Some people
see the world
with their
hearts.'

'All you have to do is keep your dreams.'

The old lady put Sally's snowball in the lake in the box where it slowly melted.

Winter came with storms that made it hard to fly, and weeks of grey skies that looked as if they would never end. Sally sat by her grandmother's bedroom window looking out at the rain. The old lady slept most of the time and when she woke up Sally read her stories.

'You know what would be wonderful right now?' said the old lady.

'What?'

'To fly away from the dead trees and all this cold, to fly into the sunshine and fields of green.'

So they did. When everyone else was asleep, Sally wrapped her grandmother up in a thick coat and scarf and they flew into the darkness of the winter night. They crossed the equator and raced the dawn around the world until they came to golden islands sitting in an endless blue sea. The old lady slept on the beach while Sally swam in the lagoon.

'If you kept flying,' said Sally as they travelled home, 'you could spend all your life in daytime.'

As the sun rose again, they flew in through the bedroom window and as everyone else woke up, they slept.

Sally's grandmother dreamt of the time she had been Sally's age and of all the wonderful places she had visited. One by one, she visited them again and when she came to her favourite place, she took her last breath and stayed there for ever.

Sally grew up but never lost her dreams. There were times when it was hard, times when it would have been easier to come down to earth and never fly again. On those days she took down her grandmother's box and trailed her fingers in the lake.

She flew with her children and when they had children of their own she flew with them too – to the rainforest, to the pyramids, to fields of snow and finally to the golden beach by the clear lagoon.

For Anne

A Random House book
Published by Random House Australia Pty Ltd
Level 3, 100 Pacific Highway, North Sydney NSW 2060
www.randomhouse.com.au

First published in the United Kingdom
by Hutchinson Children's Books 2001
This edition published by Random House Australia 2010

Addresses for companies within the Random House Group
can be found at www.randomhouse.com.au/offices.

A Cataloguing-in-Publication entry is available
from the National Library of Australia

ISBN 978 1 74166 420 1

Printed and bound by Sing Cheong Printing Co. Ltd, Hong Kong

10 9 8 7 6 5 4 3 2 1

Visit Colin Thompson's website:
http://www.colinthompson.com